OXFORD

Brothers in Arms

JULIE REEVES

Stage 4 (1400 headwords)

Illustrated by Jake Gumbleton

Series Editor: Rachel Bladon
Founder Editors: Jennifer Bassett
and Tricia Hedge

OXFORD
UNIVERSITY PRESS

Great Clarendon Street, Oxford, OX2 6DP, United Kingdom

Oxford University Press is a department of the University of Oxford.
It furthers the University's objective of excellence in research, scholarship,
and education by publishing worldwide. Oxford is a registered trade
mark of Oxford University Press in the UK and in certain other countries

This simplified edition © Oxford University Press 2018

The moral rights of the author have been asserted

First published in Oxford Bookworms 2018

10 9 8 7 6 5 4 3 2 1

No unauthorized photocopying

All rights reserved. No part of this publication may be reproduced,
stored in a retrieval system, or transmitted, in any form or by any means,
without the prior permission in writing of Oxford University Press, or as
expressly permitted by law, by licence or under terms agreed with the
appropriate reprographics rights organization. Enquiries concerning
reproduction outside the scope of the above should be sent to the ELT
Rights Department, Oxford University Press, at the address above

You must not circulate this work in any other form and you must
impose this same condition on any acquirer

Links to third party websites are provided by Oxford in good faith and
for information only. Oxford disclaims any responsibility for the materials
contained in any third party website referenced in this work

ISBN: 978 0 19 462534 0

A complete recording of this Bookworms
edition of *Brothers in Arms* is available.

Printed in China

Word count (main text): 16,143

For more information on the Oxford Bookworms Library,
visit www.oup.com/elt/gradedreaders

ACKNOWLEDGEMENTS

Illustrations by: Jake Gumbleton

*The publisher would like to thank the following for the permission to reproduce
photographs:* Getty Images p.81 (robotics museum/Greg Wood).

CONTENTS

CHAPTER ONE
The Room

Breathe deeply, Finn told himself, as the door closed behind him and the key turned in the lock. He was now alone in The Room with nothing more than four windowless walls to look at and silence to fight against. Silence was his enemy. Hours of sitting in silence made him want to scream. Sometimes he did scream, and bang on the door, too. When he was younger, he used to hope that someone would hear him and come running to help. He didn't hope any more.

Finn closed his eyes and tried to take a deep breath. Keep calm, keep calm, he said to himself. His chest felt heavy and his hands trembled. He started counting out loud: 'one, two, three'… Sometimes this helped. 'Thirty-one, thirty-two'… and sometimes it didn't.

Finn had known it was a bad idea to make trouble in Miss Edwards' class. He just couldn't stop himself.

It all began when Miss Edwards, their new teacher, told her students that she had a nice surprise for them after lunch: instead of sport in the afternoon, they would have an extra lesson of creative writing. Creative writing?! A noise escaped from Finn's chest. It sounded like an animal crying in pain. A few heads turned his way.

'Do you have a problem with that, Finn Harper?' said Miss Edwards. Her voice was sharp and cold as ice.

'No, Miss Edwards,' Finn replied.

But Finn did have a problem with it. He found creative writing very boring, and painting was even duller. It was what they did all day, every day in his school, and he was sick of it. He wanted to study maths or science like his brother Adam did, but he knew that was just a dream at Mangrove High School.

'"No"?' Miss Edwards repeated. 'Is that *all* you have to say?'

Finn knew that she was waiting for him to apologize, but he just stared back. Miss Edwards' eyes narrowed. *She looks like a cat*, Finn thought, *a rather nasty cat watching a bird land at its feet.* He didn't like her, and he wondered why she had become a teacher. From what he saw, she certainly didn't like teenagers very much.

'Well, Finn Harper, I'm waiting. You are suddenly very quiet, I see.' She was smiling at him, but her eyes were cold and hard. She was playing with him like a cat does with a small animal it has caught. 'Anyone would think I was going to eat you!'

Finn laughed so loudly that his voice seemed to echo round the walls. The picture he had imagined just a minute ago of Miss Edwards as a cat ready to draw blood – his blood – was still fresh. Could Miss Edwards read his thoughts?

Every head in the room now turned to look at him. Some of the students were silently laughing along with him, but Ellie, his best friend, wasn't one of them. She shook her head to warn him to stop, but he couldn't.

'Finn Harper, rudeness is not acceptable. In my short time at this school, you have shown yourself to be a very stupid boy. Do you think being silly and disobedient will win you friends?' Miss Edwards didn't wait for him to answer. 'Well, let me tell you, it won't. It is time, I'm afraid, to call for one of The Wardens.'

Finn put his head in his hands. Why had he made that noise? Miss Edwards was right: he was stupid. Why couldn't he be polite like other people? He used to be able to do it. Not so long ago, he was both sensible and obedient; but now, he seemed to look for trouble. Unfortunately, he always found it.

The Wardens were feared by everyone. They didn't beat you or anything like that. In fact, they almost never spoke. They just stared at you with their empty eyes, and then turned and led you away. You felt you had no choice – you had to go with them. No one ever disobeyed The Wardens. They wore white shirts, black hats, and black suits and ties, and had eyes as hard as stone, but it was their silence that made Finn feel sick. Or perhaps knowing that there was a far worse silence ahead was what put the knife of fear into him.

■ ■ ▪

'So how was The Room, bad boy?' Ellie had waited for him after school.

'Fine,' said Finn, kicking a stone along the road.

'Fine?' said Ellie. 'Are you sure about that?'

'Yeah. You know what it's like.'

'I know what it's like for *me*. And yes, *I* find it fine.' Ellie smiled and gave him a push with her shoulder. She knew

No one ever disobeyed The Wardens.

him well, too well. They'd been friends since they started school at five, and there were no secrets between them. She knew that Finn hated The Room more than anyone else.

'Why didn't I keep my big mouth shut, Ellie? The thing is, I was imagining Miss Edwards as a cat and—'

'It made you fall about laughing?' Ellie often finished Finn's sentences. She always seemed to know what he was thinking. He liked it. It made him feel safe.

'You know, Finn, you ought to avoid annoying Miss Edwards or you'll be back in The Room again tomorrow.'

'And *you're* telling *me* this? You're almost never out of it!'

It was true. Ellie had always been a rebel. She was the one who always went home dirty when they played in the woods, the one who always rode her bicycle dangerously fast, the one who cut her hair in a new way almost every month. She was also the most creative person in the school. Teachers always gave her top marks when they saw her drawings and paintings, and her stories were often read out loud as an example of how to write well. Finn knew that Ellie preferred it when the teachers didn't notice her at all. But she couldn't make herself paint a bad picture or write a boring story, and so the teachers continued to tell her what an excellent student she was. Perhaps that was why she rebelled and got sent to The Room so often. She didn't want to be too good.

'So, did you do what I told you?' Ellie said.

'What, imagine I was swimming in deep blue seas or climbing to the top of the highest mountain?' Finn laughed, though he clearly wasn't finding anything at all amusing.

'Yes,' Ellie said, 'believe me, it works. The time and the silence pass much more quickly when you can take your thoughts somewhere else, Finn. It can be restful, too, sitting there with no work to do.'

'It isn't for me!' Finn said. He was reminded of earlier that day, of how he had tried to take deep breaths as he followed The Wardens over the school field to The Room. *Don't be so silly*, he'd told himself, *it won't be so bad*, but the pain in his chest had only got worse with every step. He hated small places, and those four windowless walls seemed very close when there was no way to escape them. It was so empty in there – so very small and empty.

'Anyway,' Finn continued, unable to hide the tremble in his voice, 'why do they make us go there? It's not just to punish people like me – we all have to go sometimes,

It was so empty in The Room – so very small and empty.

whether we've done something wrong or not. You more than most.'

'Well, I think…' Ellie began. She looked at Finn, and then stopped and turned away. 'Oh, never mind.'

'What? Go on, Ellie. What were you going to say? I want to know.'

Ellie took a deep breath. 'I think they take us to The Room and put those headsets on us for a reason. In some way I don't understand, they listen in on our thoughts.' She paused and looked at Finn hard. 'That's what I think.'

'That's a bit extreme! Why would they do that?'

'Oh, I don't know. Perhaps I'm being stupid.' She started to walk quickly towards home. Finn caught up with her.

'Hey, wait! What's the hurry suddenly?'

'Nothing. I've just got some work to finish when I get home and—'

'Don't be angry, Ellie. You know I hate that school as much as you do. And to be honest, I've wondered about those headsets, too. I mean, sometimes they play music through them and sometimes not. Why do we have to wear them if there's nothing to listen to?'

'That's what I'd like to know,' said Ellie.

'Oh, I hate everything about that school! Absolutely everything. Painting, stories, more painting, more stories, that's all we do. And I hate being one of the… the…' He hesitated.

'The *what*, Finn?'

'Don't pretend you don't know, Ellie. We're in a school for the useless. It's true, isn't it? They think we're stupid, that we couldn't possibly do anything but drawing or music or writing endless stories. We aren't even allowed computers. My parents let Adam have one in his bedroom, and all of his friends have them, but, of course, they're all in Highway Academy, the school for the clever, the "chosen ones".'

Ellie's eyes narrowed, which wasn't a good sign.

'Hmm, so let's be clear, Finn. Because I like drawing and writing stories, I'm useless?'

'Sorry, Ellie, you know I don't mean it like that. You are the brightest student in the whole school! I've told you that a hundred times.'

'And?' Ellie tried to hide her smile. It was hard to stay angry with Finn.

'And what?'

'How about the prettiest, kindest, most sensitive... I could go on.' She laughed.

'Nice try, Ellie Blackstone!' smiled Finn. Then he was silent for a moment as he tried to get his thoughts in order.

'It's different for you, though, Ellie,' he said at last. 'I'm no good at all the things you can do, but I do like understanding how things work. Remember that old book we found in the library about engines and motors? I loved it. I used to read it every chance I got until it disappeared! If they would let me study maths and things like that, I know I could do really well at school.'

A shadow suddenly passed over Ellie's face. She took hold of Finn's arm, and her eyes shone a bright green. Sometimes Finn felt that he could easily fall right into them and sail into another world.

'Finn, we both know that something isn't right around here. I know that sometimes we have no choice about going to The Room, but can you be careful? I can control where my thoughts go when I'm in there, but you...' She paused.

A shadow suddenly passed over Ellie's face.

'Well, if I'm right and they *are* listening in on our thoughts, I don't think they should know what's inside your head!'

Finn knew she was right. Ellie was always right.

They walked in silence to the corner of the street where they always went their separate ways.

'See you tomorrow, Ellie.'

'Or perhaps before?'

'You mean you want to go out again? I'm not sure, Ellie. You were nearly caught last time.'

This was Finn and Ellie's great secret. For the past few months, they had been leaving their homes at night when everyone was asleep. It wasn't an easy thing to do because where they lived, all the homes were locked by *SafeHome*, the town computer system. You needed a password to open the doors after midnight, but Finn had discovered his family's password by watching very carefully every time his older brother, Adam, used it. It made Finn happy to think that Adam didn't suspect a thing. Ellie, luckily, only had to wait for her parents to fall asleep, and then she escaped through a small kitchen window which wasn't locked by *SafeHome*. The last time, however, she had knocked a cup and broken it, and the noise had nearly woken her parents up.

'I promise I won't make a noise!' Ellie gave Finn an extra big smile, knowing that Finn would not refuse her then. 'I'll throw a stone at your window. OK?'

'Fine. I'll keep my light on for you.'

Ellie waved Finn goodbye. As he watched her go, he felt his heart lift at the thought of seeing her again that night.

CHAPTER TWO

Finn's Day Gets Worse

Finn was surprised to find the house empty when he got home just after four. His parents never got back from work until six o'clock each day, but his brother was usually there. However, there was a note from Adam on the kitchen table. He had football training until 6.30, the note said, but he was going to be home for dinner. Finn was pleased, very pleased. He now had two hours on his own – and that meant that he could try once more to get onto *Serveworld* on Adam's computer!

Finn had been trying for months to discover Adam's computer password. Whenever Adam left his bedroom door open a little, Finn watched him from the landing. Keeping as quiet as he could, he studied Adam's fingers as they typed out the password, and he tried to remember exactly where Adam put them. Then, whenever Finn was alone, he put his fingers in the same places on the keyboard, choosing the letters and numbers that he thought Adam had typed.

Excitedly, Finn typed EX7*O@/. *Incorrect password* appeared on the screen on the wall in front of him. He tried again. WX7*O@/. *Incorrect password*. Finn hit the desk hard. He was mad with himself for getting it wrong again. He only had three guesses before *Serveworld* locked, so the next one was his last chance that day. His hands shook a little as he typed WZ7*O@/. The screen suddenly lit up. Finn threw his arms into the air. 'Yes, yes, yes!' he shouted. Rows of triangles and circles appeared in yellow, red, and green with lists of numbers underneath: 100, 1,000, 1,000,000, followed by $1,000,000^2$, $10,000,000^3$...

Finn sat back in the chair and stared at the numbers. What did it all mean? This was not what he expected to see. There were no words to guide him. He tried to understand what was in front of him, but it was impossible. *Oh, why did Adam have to be so clever?* A wave of jealousy washed over him, and not for the first time. Annoyingly, like all the students at Highway Academy, Adam was very clever at maths and science. He was good at sport, too. *If I could do half the things he can do, life would be so much better*, Finn thought angrily.

'What do you think you're doing?' The sound of Adam's voice made Finn jump.

'What do you think you're doing?'

'I … I thought you were at football training,' said Finn shakily.

'Clearly, or you wouldn't be spying on me.'

'I wasn't spying. I was just…' Finn didn't want to say how much he wanted to learn the things his brother knew.

'Just what? Don't pretend that you were only interested in helping me with my homework!'

Adam laughed, but Finn didn't find it at all funny. He hated it when his brother thought that he was stupid.

'So, Einstein, how did you find out my password?' Adam smiled unkindly.

'I guessed.'

'Not a good answer. The chance of guessing my password is about 1 in 218 trillion, so I think it's safe to say that you are lying.'

Finn looked at the floor. He knew how angry Adam would be if he told the truth, but he had no choice.

'I watched you typing it in, watched where your fingers were on the keyboard.'

'So, I was right. You *were* spying. I suppose now I'll have to tell Mum and Dad what you've been doing behind our backs.'

Finn knew that trying to use *Serveworld* would get him into real trouble. His parents were very strict about not letting him use it. When Finn had said to them a few times that it wasn't fair, they hadn't shouted or screamed at him, but something about their hard, cold looks had frightened him. They had made him feel like all the light was about to go out of the world. Just remembering the last time it had happened made him tremble.

'Please, Adam, please don't tell. I promise I won't do it again.'

'Why should I believe you? What other secrets have you been hiding?'

'None!' It was another lie, of course, but Finn wasn't going to tell his brother about his plan to meet Ellie that night. If his parents found out about that, they would change the *SafeHome* password. Then he would never be able to get out at night again.

'Honestly, Adam. I'm telling you the truth. I have no more secrets. Listen, if you don't tell Mum and Dad, I'll clean your bedroom for the next month.' Finn looked around at the tidy room. 'Or bring you breakfast in bed at the weekend,' he added hurriedly.

Adam opened his mouth to speak, but hesitated. He brushed his fingers through his hair and looked thoughtfully at Finn.

'OK. If you promise me you're telling the truth.'

'I promise.'

And with that, Adam stood away from the door and let Finn escape to his room.

Finn was surprised that Adam had let him go so easily. Was Adam playing a game with him? Perhaps when their parents got home, Adam would tell them everything after all! It wouldn't be the first time that he had made trouble for Finn.

It seemed a very long time until six o'clock. Finn looked out of the window every few minutes, although he knew that his parents, like all the neighbours, returned at the exact same time every day. He and Ellie couldn't understand how the whole town could do the same boring stuff all the time. Everyone worked the same hours at the same company, and lived in the same kind of house with the same rows of flowers in their very tidy gardens. Ellie said that when she grew up, she wanted to live somewhere wild, somewhere hidden deep in a dark forest away from order and routine. Finn hoped with all his heart that she would want him to live there, too.

At last, Finn heard the sound of car doors shutting and a key turning in the lock.

'Hi, boys!'

Finn's parents came upstairs to say hello to the two boys, but it was clear immediately that it was Finn they wanted to talk to.

'Well, son, we've heard that you were sent to The Room again. Sit down and tell us all about it.'

Finn felt miserable. He knew what was going to happen. It was the same each time: he described every detail of his time in The Room and they asked question after question. 'What were you thinking then, Finn?' 'Did you feel angry or sad?' 'Why did you imagine sailing on a boat?' 'Did that help you feel less frightened?' The questions kept coming, until he started to feel like he was back in there. As usual, his parents didn't ask him why he'd been sent to The Room for behaving badly. They never got angry about that. But when he didn't want to answer any more questions, they gave him that awful, icy look that he hated.

The questions kept coming...

Finn was exhausted by the time his parents had finished questioning him, so he was quiet through dinner. Adam was too, but that wasn't unusual. Finn was always asked about his school day and his friends, but he had noticed recently that his parents didn't show as much interest in Adam. Finn didn't understand why this was. Adam's school day was much more interesting than his own. Adam was much cleverer, but they were always so delighted with every silly drawing Finn brought home. How could his parents be so insensitive? Sometimes, Finn felt sorry for Adam, although he knew it wasn't a good idea to show it, or to try and talk about it with him. In fact, Adam didn't like Finn to talk to him about anything much. It made Finn feel very lonely at times.

That night, Finn lay on his bed listening for the sound of a stone on his window. After the day he'd had, he was very tired, but he was also hungry for excitement. With any luck, he and Ellie would soon be alone in the cool night air. Finn smiled at the thought – it was going to be the best kind of end to a difficult day.

CHAPTER THREE
Finn and Ellie's Adventure

Finn and Ellie knew the routine. They said nothing to each other when they met behind the trees at the end of Everglades Avenue, and they stayed in the shadows as they moved along the streets towards the edge of town. At last, when there were no more houses, and the woods rose around them, Finn whispered to Ellie, 'You took your time!'

'Yeah, I planned to come sooner, but Mum and Dad were awake for ever! I could hear them talking in their bedroom. They don't usually stay up late, so I made sure they were asleep before I left. I almost fell asleep myself while I was waiting for them to stop!'

'Me too! It was a long day.'

Ellie smiled. 'Did your parents give you a hard time with all their usual questions?'

'What do *you* think?' said Finn, and Ellie knew it was better not to ask him anything more. They walked on silently for a while, and then Ellie suddenly stopped and turned to Finn.

'You know, Mum and Dad weren't just talking; they were... well, kind of *arguing*.'

'Arguing?' Finn was surprised. 'Are you sure?'

Ellie nodded. Finn didn't know what to say. He'd never heard his own parents argue, and Ellie always said her parents didn't either.

'What were they arguing about?'

'I don't know. I stayed in my room. I didn't want to get caught. If they'd found me listening at their door, I wouldn't be here with you now!'

'Yes, I suppose you're right.' Finn was thinking about earlier that day when Adam found him at his computer. One word from Adam to their parents about that and Finn wouldn't be going out on night-time adventures with Ellie again. He wanted to tell Ellie all about what had happened, but this didn't seem the right time.

'I couldn't believe they were arguing,' Ellie went on. 'They agree about everything. Like yours do.' She paused. 'Don't you think that's strange?'

'Arguing?'

'No, *agreeing*, stupid! I mean, *all* the time.'

Ellie was right. Finn did think it was a little strange. He'd thought so for a while now. After all, he often argued with Ellie, and she was his closest, dearest friend. He and Adam argued, too. They didn't use to, but in the last couple of years, they had argued a lot.

'Yes, I guess it is strange,' he said as he walked ahead, 'but let's just have some fun tonight, OK?'

Finn started to walk more quickly, putting a distance between him and Ellie. He'd had a difficult day and he didn't want any more problems to think about.

Ellie nodded and followed. Finn noticed, though, that she was biting her lip. When Ellie bit her lip, it was a sure sign that she was worried about something. Very worried.

The churchyard they were aiming for about a kilometre or more outside the town. They weren't allowed to go there. But when Finn and Ellie had found it, they had fallen in love with the place at once. It was so quiet and old. All the buildings in their town were quite new; the churchyard was the only place with some history. Best of all, no one went there any more. The door of the church was locked and most of the windows were broken. Finn and Ellie had tried many times to break open the door, but it was made of thick wood and as hard as rock to move. Birds were the only living things that could see inside the church now.

They slowed down as they came close to the walls of the churchyard, and looked around them. Although they had never seen anybody on these night-time adventures, they always checked that they were alone. The sound of the wind in the trees, the banging of the broken gate, the awful screams of cats fighting in the woods around the churchyard – any of these things could make them jump with fear. When they first started escaping to the churchyard, they had told each other ghost stories. Neither of them believed in ghosts, but it was still frightening to talk about them in a churchyard at midnight. They had soon agreed to stop.

'Everything seems fine,' Ellie said, looking around. 'Shall we go in?'

Finn's eyes slid over the graves and between the trees.

'Yeah, OK with me.'

They made their way to their favourite place in the far corner of the churchyard.

'Have you brought—' Finn began, but Ellie already knew what he was about to ask.

'Everything seems fine,' Ellie said, looking around.

'Anything to eat? Yes, I've brought some chocolate cake. Oh, and an apple. Are you hungry?' said Ellie. 'Silly question; you're always hungry!' She took some chocolate cake from her bag and passed it to him.

For a few minutes, the only noise they could hear was the sound of each other eating. When they had finished, Ellie started biting her lip again.

'Have you ever wondered, Finn, why there are no graves here from the last twenty years?'

Finn laughed. 'You mean you've looked at every one?'

'Yes.'

'Oh, come on. That can't be true.'

'If you don't believe me, take a look.' Finn didn't move. 'The thing is,' she continued, 'you don't have to look. When was the last time someone you know died?'

'My grandparents died a long time before I was born,' Finn replied.

'Mine too. Aunts and uncles? Cousins?'

'They live in America.'

'Mine are in Australia. Do you ever get to see them?'

Finn shook his head. His mouth suddenly felt dry.

'And the people at school... none of them have grandparents either,' Ellie added.

'How do you know?'

'Have you ever heard anyone talk about their family visiting? Or a grandparent being sick? Or an uncle dying?'

'What are you saying, Ellie?'

'It's strange, that's what I'm saying. And do you know what else is strange?'

'No, but I know you're going to tell me.'

'Why do none of the people from our school ever come back after they leave for work or college or move away?'

'Would you want to come back here?!'

'That's not what I'm saying. Most of those who go to Highway Academy return after college, don't they? They go to work, marry. But the ones who leave Mangrove High School – they never come back.'

Finn said nothing for a moment. These questions had always been in his mind, but he had never wanted to ask them. Now Ellie was making him think about them. 'What do you think it means, then?' he said at last. 'Where do they all go?'

'I've been thinking about it a lot—' Ellie began, but then she stopped and looked around. 'Did you hear that?' she whispered.

Finn nodded. He put his finger to his lips to warn her not to speak. They looked around, searching for any movement. There was none.

'It was just branches waving in the wind,' said Finn. 'You know how ghostly that can sound.'

Ellie didn't look so sure. Finn could feel her tremble against his shoulder.

'Are you OK? You're—'

'I'm fine, just a bit cold,' Ellie said quickly.

'Here, borrow my coat.' Finn knew Ellie wasn't cold, but he enjoyed taking care of her – when she let him! But as Finn started to take his coat off, Ellie breathed in sharply.

'Look over there!'

Finn's eyes followed the path of Ellie's finger. Clouds had just passed in front of the moon, so it was difficult to see. Was that a figure moving behind the graves, or shadows?

Finn wasn't sure, but he didn't want to find out.

'Quick, Ellie, let's get out of here!'

He took her hand and pulled her to her feet. Together they jumped over the wall and ran as fast as their legs could take them. Every few seconds, they looked over their shoulders to see if anyone was following. The road was empty and seemed very, very long, but although they had to go slower when they got into town, they didn't stop running until they reached the corner where they usually separated.

'I'll walk you home,' Finn whispered, after his breathing had calmed.

'No, I'm fine.'

'Ellie, please,' Finn said.

'No. I want you to go home.'

Finn could see that Ellie meant what she said.

'Well, if you're sure. But—'

'Be careful. Yes, I will, I promise. You too.' Ellie gave him a smile.

Finn had a million things he wanted to talk to her about. Who, or what, was in the churchyard? Was someone spying on them? If so, who? It clearly wasn't the police because they wouldn't hide behind graves. The questions would have to wait until tomorrow, though. It wasn't safe to be out any longer.

'Goodnight, Finn.'

'Goodnight, Ellie. Sleep well.'

She turned and ran into the night. Finn watched her disappear before turning towards home.

CHAPTER FOUR
Where is Ellie?

Finn didn't sleep much that night. Worries filled his head. Had Ellie got home without any problem? If she hadn't, there would be trouble. He imagined all kinds of punishments for her. And for him as well. Then there were all those things Ellie had been talking about, too. There was so much to think about. Finn finally fell asleep just before his alarm rang.

His parents noticed the dark rings under his eyes immediately.

Finn's parents noticed the dark rings under his eyes immediately.

'Are you sick, Finn?' his mum asked at breakfast.

'No, I'm fine.'

'You don't look fine,' his dad said.

'Perhaps you should have a day off school,' said Adam.

Three pairs of eyes turned to look at Finn's brother. It wasn't like Adam to suggest a thing like that. He hated it when Finn was sick and allowed to stay at home. Adam never got ill, and so never had time off school.

'No, I'm fine, really. I want to go to school.'

All eyes now turned on Finn. It wasn't often he surprised his family.

'We should take his temperature,' said Adam. 'If he's refusing to stay at home, he must have a fever!'

'Yes, you're right, Adam. I'll do that,' his mum said. Finn's parents never seemed to understand when someone was joking.

'It's OK, Mum, there's no need. I don't feel sick at all and anyway there's...' Finn hesitated, 'some homework I really want to finish.'

His dad stared at him for a moment like he was looking at a painting for the first time. Finn was used to it: both his parents often stared at him. He just had to wait for the moment to pass.

'Well done, Finn,' his dad said, finally. 'We're pleased you're showing an interest in your studies.'

'Thanks, Dad. I'm trying, I really am.'

He avoided looking at Adam when he said that. In fact, he avoided looking at him during the rest of breakfast. Adam had been behaving so strangely lately. It was difficult to judge sometimes whether he was going to be nasty or nice. Finn was used to Adam being nasty. It was when Adam was nice that Finn got worried.

Finn was desperate to get to school to check if Ellie was OK. He also wanted to discuss what had happened last night.

But Finn didn't have the chance to talk to Ellie because she wasn't at school.

He didn't hear a word his teacher said all morning. He was too busy thinking about why Ellie wasn't there. Had her parents found out and locked her in her bedroom? Had she been attacked on the way home? Oh, why hadn't he walked home with her and made sure she was OK?

At lunchtime, Finn decided to go to Ellie's house. No one was allowed to leave school during the day. The teachers were very strict about it, and if you were caught, you got sent to The Room. Ellie had said he should avoid The Room from now on. He knew she was right, but he was too worried to wait until the end of the day to see her. It was worth a try.

After he'd eaten, he made his way to the far edge of the school field. There were plenty of trees there, so he could easily hide. He'd also noticed that the teachers didn't spend too much time walking around that part of the school. If he could manage to get there without anyone seeing him, it would be very easy, he thought, to climb over the wall. It was only five minutes to Ellie's house if he ran all the way. He could get there and back before anyone noticed he was missing.

All went well. He moved from one group of students to another until he got close to the wooded corner of the field. Then, after checking no one was watching, he ran to the safety of the trees. It was quiet and dark there. He waited a moment to make sure he hadn't been followed, and then began climbing the wall. It wasn't quite as easy as he had thought. It was higher than he remembered. He tried again and again to climb up. It wasn't long before his fingers began to bleed.

Adam would have no problem climbing this, he thought angrily. Then aloud he said, 'Why am I so useless?'

'Why indeed?'

Finn looked down. Miss Edwards was standing there with two Wardens by her side. He'd been so busy trying to climb the wall that he hadn't heard them come close.

'I think a visit to The Room will now be necessary, Finn Harper,' she said. 'It's becoming quite a habit, isn't it?'

There was nothing Finn could do. Angrily, he let himself drop to the grass below, and The Wardens took his arms and marched him to the place he feared most.

It was harder for him this time. The fear and worry he already felt got worse as soon as the door to The Room was locked. Unusually, The Room was dark and there was a strange kind of music playing. It was awful. He put his hands over his ears under the headset and tried not to listen, but the noise seemed to get louder. His heart started beating faster and he banged on the door. 'Let me out!' he shouted, again and again.

■ ■ ■

Finn tried again and again to climb up.

Finn woke up in bed at home, and his parents were standing over him, watching. He had no idea how or when he had got there. The last thing he remembered was banging on the door in The Room.

'How are you feeling, Finn?' his mum asked.

'Fine,' he replied, though he wasn't sure if this was really the truth.

'The school tells us you have had a tough time in The Room,' his dad said.

'I don't remember.'

'Really?' His mum bent closer to his face. 'Are you sure, Finn? Don't you remember anything at all?'

So it's already started, thought Finn. *I've only just woken up and the questions have begun.*

He was right. The questions came one after the other. 'What were you thinking about before you fainted?' 'Did you have bad thoughts?' 'Did you imagine you were somewhere else?' 'Who were you with?' 'Were you feeling happy?' On and on the questions came until Finn had had enough. He needed time to think, and to understand – about Ellie, and about the things they had talked about in the churchyard.

'Leave me alone!' he screamed. 'Get out and leave me alone!'

His parents looked at each other and then at Finn. They seemed confused. They weren't angry, although he had shouted at them. Why did they never get angry? Why, when he felt like he was going to explode, did they stay so calm?

'Very well, Finn. We'll leave you to rest. We'll talk again later when you feel better.'

A few minutes later, Adam appeared. He came into Finn's room and closed the door behind him.

'So I hear you fainted in The Room?' He was smiling. It was a surprisingly kind smile.

Finn nodded.

'You really can't remember anything?'

'No!'

'Not even what you were thinking—'

'Oh, not you as well!' Finn shouted. 'I've had enough of

all these questions.'

'Shh,' whispered Adam, 'you don't want to bring Mum and Dad back, do you?'

Finn shook his head and Adam sat down on the bed. Finn stared at his brother.

'Don't be so alarmed,' Adam said. 'I just wanted to have a little talk with you.'

'A little talk?'

'Is that so surprising?'

'Well, yes, it is.'

Adam's expression changed. He didn't look so friendly any more. He got up to leave.

'No, don't go,' Finn said. 'I'm sorry. Please stay. I was wondering if you could help me with something.'

Adam's eyes grew wider. He wasn't used to Finn asking him for anything, and certainly not for help. But Finn had spent every waking moment worrying about Ellie. He had a feeling that something awful had happened to her. He couldn't possibly wait until the next day to find out if he was right. The only person he could turn to was his brother. The question was, how much could he trust him?

'Well?' Adam was watching him carefully.

'It's Ellie...' Finn stopped. He couldn't tell Adam about last night. If Adam told their parents about *Serveworld* and leaving the house at night, who knows how they would punish him.

'She wasn't in school today and I need to ask her about some homework. Could you find out if she's sick?'

Adam laughed, though he didn't really look amused.

'Ellie, Ellie, always Ellie! You're so fond of her, but she'll lead you into trouble one of these days.'

Finn felt his face turn red. Adam got up to leave.

'If she's not in school, Finn, she must be sick, don't you think?'

'Yes, I suppose. I just wondered when she'd be back.'

'You'll find out tomorrow, I imagine,' Adam said as he walked to the door.

'Please, Adam,' Finn called. 'Will you find out for me?' His eyes had begun to fill with tears.

Adam turned. Finn expected him to make a joke or say something nasty about him crying. Instead, he nodded.

'OK. If she's so important to you, I'll find out.' He turned to leave.

'Adam?' Finn called.

'Yes?'

'You wanted to speak to me about something?'

Adam looked at him hard. 'It doesn't matter,' he said finally. And with that, he left Finn alone.

Finn lay back on the bed. Why was Adam being so nice to him lately? It was strange. Adam was strange. At times, he seemed just like their parents, very controlled and calm, with that distant look in his eyes. Recently, though, there had been more and more moments when Adam had been angry or nasty or had even made Finn laugh.

Finn closed his eyes. Adam was another mystery to add to his growing list.

CHAPTER FIVE

The Men in Suits

Adam kept his promise to bring news about Ellie. Less than half an hour after their conversation, he returned to Finn's bedroom and told him Ellie had a bad cold. Finn wasn't happy, though. He wasn't sure whether to believe Adam. How had he been able to find out about Ellie so quickly? He still suspected that Adam was playing some kind of game with him. Was Adam waiting for the perfect time to get him into trouble? The truth was, he didn't trust his brother. In fact, he was beginning to question who – or even what – he could trust.

When Ellie came back to school the next day, Finn was very relieved. Thankfully, she was safe, although clearly she had a terrible cold. So Adam had been telling the truth after all.

As soon as Finn saw her, he ran to meet her.

'I wouldn't come near me if I were you!' she said, pointing at her red nose and watery eyes.

Finn laughed. 'I missed you too!' he said.

Finn expected Ellie to reply to his joke with another one, but she didn't. Instead, she pulled him to one side and made sure no one could hear her.

'Meet me over by the football field at lunchtime. I have something I need to tell you.'

'What is it?'

'I can't tell you now. It's too dangerous.'

'Dangerous? What do you mean?'

'I mean, I've discovered some stuff that none of us should know about. It's frightening, Finn. Really frightening. I don't quite understand it yet. I need to find out more. But if they discover how much I know, I'll be in great danger.'

'What do you mean, *they*? Is—'

'Ellie Blackstone and Finn Harper, stop talking and get to your lesson. You're going to be late!'

'Yes, Miss Edwards,' Ellie said without looking up.

They walked towards the door to the classroom.

'Are you OK?' Finn had noticed that when Miss Edwards appeared, Ellie's face turned white. She was trembling, too.

'I'm fine, Finn. Just meet me at lunchtime. All right? And don't get sent to The Room. Promise me.'

'Ellie, you're frightening me. What's going on?'

'You should be frightened, Finn. We should all be very, very frightened. Shh now, go to your seat; Miss Edwards is staring at us.'

Time had never passed so slowly as it did that morning. Finn couldn't stop himself looking over at Ellie. She seemed to be behaving normally, but Finn knew better. Her book was open in front of her, but the pages didn't turn often. She didn't put her hand up to answer any questions either. More importantly, she bit her lip the whole time. Finn expected to see a drop of blood fall onto the desk any minute.

When the bell sounded for lunch, Finn was the first out of his seat. He was about to step into the hall, but he found two men in dark suits standing in his way.

'Move to one side, boy,' said one. Finn didn't need the

man to ask him a second time.

Finn watched as the men went over to speak to Miss Edwards. It was a short conversation. Miss Edwards pointed at Ellie, and the men turned to look at her. The next few seconds were like watching a film, but with time slowed down. Finn saw Ellie's eyes grow wide with horror as the men came closer. All the other students watched, too. The silence was heavy, and the hairs on the back of Finn's neck rose. It was clear that the men were not interested in a friendly talk about Ellie's creative writing. *Run, Ellie*, Finn thought. *Please, just run*! But Ellie didn't run. She put down her books and left the room, with one man on each side of her.

'Ellie!' Finn called, but she stared ahead as she walked, and didn't look at him once.

As soon as she left the building, everyone started speaking all at once. 'Who are those men?' 'Where are they taking Ellie?' 'Is Ellie in trouble?' Because he was Ellie's best friend, people started turning to Finn for the answers, but Finn didn't have any. In fact, he had far more questions than any of them could imagine.

'I don't know. I don't know anything!' he shouted at them and ran outside.

He was just in time to see Ellie and the two men stop at a parked car. The car was long and black, but Finn couldn't see if there was anyone inside because the windows were made of dark glass. One of the men in suits opened a door, and Ellie was about to climb in when she suddenly turned and started to run. For a second, Finn was filled with hope, but it was soon destroyed. The men's hands immediately shot out and grabbed Ellie's arms.

Finn watched, helpless, as Ellie was pushed into the back of the car. Seconds later, the car drove away at speed, the sound of its wheels echoing in his ears. Mad with fear for Ellie, he started to run after them. He followed the car out into the road, screaming Ellie's name as loud as he could as he watched it disappear. Perhaps that was why he didn't hear The Wardens' boots coming up behind him. It was his turn to feel strong hands grab him by the arms.

The men's hands immediately shot out
and grabbed Ellie's arms.

■ ■ ▪

The Room was different from all the other times he'd been
in there. Coloured lights danced around the walls, and the
headset they put on him played the most beautiful music he
had ever heard. He closed his eyes and tried not to listen.
Ellie had told him not to get sent to The Room, but here
he was again. He owed it to her to keep control of his
thoughts. *Don't think anything*, he told himself, again and
again. *Empty your mind of every thought.* But this was
easier said than done. He tried and tried not to think of
Ellie or the men in suits or where Ellie had been taken. He
tried, but he failed. The music was so lovely and the colours
so warm on his face that his mind began to return to Ellie
again and again. And when he started smelling something
sweet – something like fresh bread and summer roses – he
lost control completely.

> *Finn enters a dream world. It is nice at first. He sees
> himself with Ellie. They are five or six years old. She
> is counting her sweets: one for him, one for her. She
> smiles as she gives him the extra one...*
>
> *Now they are eleven years old and they are climbing
> trees. Ellie climbs higher than him. She is laughing
> because he is much more careful than her. He feels sad,
> but then her foot catches on a branch. She is about to
> fall, but he grabs her arm and saves her...*
>
> *And then the dream grows darker. It is the present.
> He can see Ellie, but he isn't with her. She is in a prison
> or a hospital. There are people in white coats working
> on computers. He can hear crying in other rooms. Ellie*

looks small and frightened. He would like to reach out and touch her, but he knows he can't.

Just then, there is a loud noise and everything goes black. There is smoke everywhere. Finn can hear gunshots and the sound of running feet. Screams and shouts come from all around. He tries to call Ellie's name, but he has no voice. He tries again... nothing. And then there is only silence.

Screams and shouts come from all around.

When Finn woke up, he was in his own bed at home. His curtains were closed and he couldn't hear anyone moving around in the house. He looked at his clock on the bedside table. It was after midnight, but he couldn't remember coming home from school, having dinner with his family, going to bed, or anything.

He lay there a moment, breathing deeply, and tried to remember what had happened in the lost hours. Slowly, his mind started to clear. He saw the men in suits, Ellie trying to escape, and then the dreams he had had in The Room. Were they only dreams, he asked himself, or had he been seeing things that were really happening? *I've got to get out of here,* he thought. *I've got to try and find Ellie.*

He dressed as quickly and as quietly as he could. After putting some warm clothes in a bag, he slowly opened the door. He paused to listen for any sounds. His family were always in bed by ten o'clock, but he didn't want to take any chances. When he was sure that nobody was still up, he stepped onto the landing.

'Where do you think you're going?'

The voice was only a whisper, but the sound of it hit Finn like a shot of electricity. From the shadows, a figure appeared.

It was Adam.

CHAPTER SIX

Finn Gets Some Answers

Finn gasped. He couldn't see Adam's face, but he knew that it was him.

'Go back into your room,' Adam said quietly.

Finn shook his head. He was angry, really angry. So he'd been right after all – he couldn't trust Adam.

'You once accused me of spying,' Finn whispered, 'but it's you who's the spy!'

'Don't be stupid, Finn.'

'I'm not stupid and I'm not going back in there.'

'Oh yes you are,' said Adam.

Finn turned towards the stairs and began to run, but Adam was quicker and stronger. He grabbed Finn's arm and pushed him back into the room before he'd got even a few steps away. Adam shut the door quietly behind them.

'Sit down and keep quiet, Finn.'

'Make me!' Finn hissed.

Finn hit out at Adam, but Adam caught Finn's hand before it made contact with his chin. His fingers fastened around Finn's wrist.

'Let go; you're hurting me!' said Finn, his voice rising.

'Only if you'll be quiet!'

'So I suppose you're… you're going to…' Finn hesitated.

'I'm going to what?' said Adam, quietly. 'Tell our parents that you're about to run away?'

'Let go; you're hurting me!' said Finn, his voice rising.

'Yes,' replied Finn, but he was no longer sure what Adam was planning to do.

'Really? That's what you think? Aren't you wondering why I haven't called our parents for help yet?'

Finn nodded slowly. Adam let go of his wrist and sat down on the floor, next to the bed.

'Oh Finn, can't you see I'm trying to help you?'

Finn didn't speak. His eyes rested for a moment on the door.

'Go, then,' said Adam, sharply. 'If you don't trust me, you'd better go.' But his voice, though angry, was also touched with sadness. Finn didn't know what to think or do. Was Adam telling the truth? Did he really want to help him? If so, why? He moved slowly towards the door, watching Adam the whole time. Adam didn't move. Their eyes were fixed on each other for what seemed like minutes.

'You'd better decide what you want to do, Finn,' said Adam, in a whisper. 'We haven't got a lot of time.'

'What do you mean, "we"?'

'If you want to escape, you're going to need my help.'

'How do you know I want to escape?' hissed Finn. 'Why were you waiting outside my door? What do you know about any of this?'

Once he'd started asking questions, he realized there were a lot more he wanted answers to.

'We really haven't got time, Finn. We need to go. We're already later than I'd hoped.'

'I'm not going anywhere with you until you explain what you know and how you know it.'

Adam sighed. 'All right, Finn, you win. I'll try to explain as much as I can. You're not going to like it, though.'

Finn sat on the floor opposite his brother. His heart was beating fast. He had a feeling that the next few minutes were going to be important. He had no idea that they were going to change his life.

'Ellie was taken away yesterday, wasn't she?' said Adam gently.

Finn nodded.

'She'd found something out, right?'

'Yes,' said Finn, his eyes locked on Adam's.

'Have you any idea what it was?'

'No.' Finn's mouth was so dry, it wasn't easy to speak. 'Have you?'

'I'm afraid so.' Adam took a deep breath, and lowered his voice again. 'We're part of an experiment, Finn.'

'An experiment? What do you mean?'

'You, me, Ellie, all the other children, we're all in the biggest experiment the world has ever known.'

Finn stared at his brother and smiled. 'Oh, come on, Adam. Do you really expect me to believe that?'

'I'm serious, Finn. You haven't heard of androids, have you?'

'Androids? No. What are they?'

'They look like humans, Finn. In fact, you wouldn't be able to see the difference between an android and a human. But inside an android, there is a computer. Instead of a mind that loves and hates, there is only a computer. So an android feels nothing naturally, and has no real emotions.'

Finn put his head in his hands for a moment. Surely Adam was crazy, he thought.

'Have you ever wondered about our parents, Finn?'

'What do you mean?'

'Well, do they seem strange to you in any way?'

'No! Well, yes. I suppose. They're a bit "cold", aren't they? They never argue or anything like that, but neither do any other parents I know.'

'Doesn't that seem a bit strange to you? I mean, *we* argue a lot. You even argue with Ellie, and we all know what you feel about her!'

Finn turned bright red when Adam mentioned Ellie, but he said nothing. He was too busy thinking about his mum and dad. He'd been thinking about them a lot recently, and asking himself why he didn't feel very much for them at all. He sometimes wondered if he even loved them. They'd given him a home, food, and taken care of him. They'd shown an interest in his friends and school life, but he just didn't feel close to them. He didn't like thinking that way. He hadn't even said anything about it to Ellie, and he usually told her everything. And now, here was Adam talking about them in a way which made his stomach turn to water.

'What exactly are you trying to say, Adam? That our parents are actually – machines? – androids??' Finn attempted to laugh, but no sound came out of his mouth.

'Shh, Finn. Not too loud! Yes. That's absolutely what I'm saying.'

'You're crazy!'

'I wish I was. All the parents in the town are androids, the teachers, too, the doctors, the police – all the adults...' Adam paused. He looked uncomfortable. 'That's what Ellie found out. Not about the parents, but the teachers. She discovered they are androids and that we are part of an experiment.'

Finn stared at Adam. He didn't know whether to laugh, cry, or run away as fast as his legs could carry him.

'This is a joke, right?' Finn hoped more than anything that Adam would say yes. But he knew in his heart that Adam was telling the truth. He fell silent for a moment and tried to understand what he'd just heard. It seemed impossible.

'So how do *you* know all this?' Finn said finally. 'And if this is true, why haven't you told me before now?'

Finn knew in his heart that Adam was telling the truth.

'I didn't tell you because it was dangerous to know. I didn't want you to think about it when you were in The Room.'

'So they do listen in on our thoughts when we're in there?'

Adam nodded. 'Yes. That's why I've been planning our escape since your adventure with Ellie the other night.'

'What do you know about that?' said Finn, a little too loudly.

'Shh,' said Adam, putting his finger to his lips. 'I followed you... Don't look at me like that, Finn. I needed to make sure you were safe.'

'Safe from what? Our parents?'

'Not exactly. You see, the National Home Guard were close to the churchyard that night.'

'The army? Why?'

'Because the rebels are starting to attack places close to our town.'

Finn's mouth fell open. 'Rebels? What are you talking about?'

'There are a group of us who have decided to fight, Finn. We don't want the kind of world where androids can do experiments on people. We've started to win back villages and towns and—'

'Wait, stop right there! You're involved in all this? You've been fighting for these rebels?'

'No, not yet, but I help in other ways,' Adam said hurriedly. 'Just listen, Finn. We haven't got a lot of time. The night you left the house, I couldn't sleep. I heard you get up and I wanted to know what you were going to do. I followed you to the churchyard and got close enough to hear what you were saying…'

'So that was you we saw running among the graves?'

'Yes, Finn, it was me. I'm sorry I frightened you. I was frightened myself. After listening to you and Ellie, it was clear to me that you were starting to ask too many questions. I was worried that if you started asking the wrong people those kind of questions, you would get into trouble. Serious trouble. I decided I needed to plan our escape. But then Ellie was taken away and you spent another afternoon in The Room. I knew we had to do something tonight. I've been outside your room waiting for you to wake up. I knew you'd go looking for Ellie.'

'You still haven't told me what the experiment is, or how you got to know about it. And where are the rebels? Are they coming to help us soon?'

'Shh,' Adam bent his head to one side and listened. 'Did you hear something?' he whispered. Finn shook his head.

'We'll wait a minute and then I'll check everything is OK to leave.'

Finn opened his mouth to speak, but Adam put his hand over it. 'No more questions now. I'll tell you more later. I promise.'

For the first time in his life, Finn believed Adam.

CHAPTER SEVEN

The Escape

It was strange leaving the house at night with Adam. It was good to have his brother as a companion, though. Finn was glad he could trust him – and he *needed* to trust him. In the last hour, his world had been turned upside down, and without Adam, he would be completely alone. Finn had never imagined for one minute that his 'parents' were not human. Although he and Ellie had had questions and doubts about their life in the town, they hadn't considered this! Part of him was so angry and upset that he wanted to just sit down and cry. The other part wanted to get as far away from 'home' as possible.

'Come on, Finn,' Adam whispered, 'we've got to get out of here as soon as we can.'

Luckily, it was a cloudy night and the moon was hidden as they walked out of the town. It made Finn feel safer. When he thought that in every house in the town there were androids, his blood ran cold. He was afraid that one of them would wake up and see him and Adam leave. What would happen to them if they were caught? Adam had said that androids didn't feel, that they had no real emotions. Did that mean their 'parents' felt nothing for him? Would they find it easy to kill? Would it be easy to kill their own 'children'?

As soon as they left the town behind, Adam started to run. Finn followed, although he couldn't go as fast as Adam. He had always known that Adam was excellent at sport, but he hadn't realized before just how good he was. His brother was a fantastic runner, and so quiet, too. He moved like a cat through the night while Finn ran behind breathless.

After a while, Adam stopped and waited for Finn to catch up with him.

'Can't you run any faster?'

'No, I can't!' said Finn, breathing heavily.

'We've got quite a long way to go yet, and we need to get as far as we can before first light. They'll look for us as soon as they see we're missing.'

'Where exactly are we going, Adam? Do you know where Ellie is?'

'I've made plans to meet the rebels at a lake. From there, they'll take us to a rebel city where we'll be safe. Well, safer than here. And no, I don't know where Ellie is, Finn. I'm sorry. I'm hoping we can find out when we get to the rebel city.'

Finn was disappointed, tired, and confused, but he ran as fast as he could. He desperately wanted to reach the meeting place because he was hoping to get some more answers from Adam and the rebels. The problem was, he soon became so exhausted that he couldn't go on. He had a pain in his side so sharp that it felt like a knife was cutting into him.

'I'm sorry, Adam, I can't run any more,' Finn called to his brother. 'You'll have to carry on without me.'

'Don't be silly,' said Adam. 'I'm not leaving you here. I don't know what they'll do to you if you're caught.'

'I'll have to take that chance. I can't go as fast as you,

Adam, and if you wait for me, they'll catch us both.'

'That's not going to happen. I'll carry you on my back – end of problem.'

'Now you're being crazy again!'

'No, I'm not. I'm strong, really strong,' said Adam. 'Climb on and you'll see.' Adam bent his knees and Finn put his arms around his brother's neck.

'Ready? Off we go!'

Finn couldn't believe how fast Adam could move while carrying him. On through the night he ran across fields and rivers without ever needing to rest. Indeed, as the time

Finn couldn't believe how fast Adam could move while carrying him.

rushed by, Finn began to wonder how Adam could do it. This wasn't normal, was it? More than that, it wasn't natural. Fear started to grab hold of his thoughts. Was this plan to escape really a trap?

'Stop! I want to get off,' said Finn as they entered a forest.

'What?' said Adam. 'No resting yet, Finn. We need to keep going a bit longer. It'll be morning soon.'

'I don't care!' Finn felt suddenly very angry. If he was going to die, he wanted to know the truth first. Adam stopped and let Finn slide to the ground.

'What's the problem, Finn?' Adam looked anxious. Finn had never seen him like that before.

'You know very well what the problem is.'

Adam shook his head.

'You asked me earlier if there was anything strange about our "parents",' Finn said. 'Well, you forgot to say that there's something strange about you, too!'

'Let's not discuss this now. Please, Finn. We haven't got time.'

'Time for what? To lead me into a trap?'

'A trap? What are you talking about? Did you not believe anything I said about our parents being androids?'

'Yes, I believed you, but it's the rest of the truth I'm interested in now. Isn't it strange that you failed to mention that you are an android, too!'

Adam's chin fell to his chest.

'What's wrong, Adam? Are you feeling ashamed about lying? Oh, sorry, my mistake: you can't feel anything because you are a machine!'

Adam lifted his head and looked at Finn.

'Is that what you think of me? I'm just a machine to you?' he said softly.

'I don't think anything about you, or "Mum" and "Dad". But I do *feel* something, and what I feel is hate. I hate you, I hate them, I hate you all!'

Finn didn't wait for Adam to reply. He turned and ran deeper into the forest as quickly as he could. Tears ran down his face. *I hate him, I hate him*, he said to himself as he ran through the trees. He could hear Adam calling his name, and the sound of dry wood breaking under his feet. The sky was starting to get lighter. How long did he have before Adam or some other android caught him? *Think carefully*, he told himself; *find someplace to hide*. He didn't care about his own life any more. What mattered to him was Ellie. She was the only person he had left. He needed to stay alive if he wanted to find her.

'Finn, come back! I'm not going to hurt you. Please believe me,' Adam called.

Finn could hear him getting closer. And there was another noise, too: the sound of an engine of some kind. Finn looked up through the trees, but could see nothing. It didn't seem loud enough for a helicopter. In fact, it sounded more like a very large insect searching for food. Whatever it was, he knew that it was looking for him. As he stopped to catch his breath and decide which way to go, Adam came crashing through the trees. Finn tried to run, but Adam was far too quick for him and knocked him to the ground.

'Get off me!' Finn screamed, hitting Adam as hard as

Finn tried to run, but Adam was far too quick for him.

he could. It had no effect at all. Adam calmly grabbed his wrists and held him still.

'Shh, Finn! Don't you realize they're out there right now hunting us like wild animals?'

'Hunting *me*, you mean. You're one of them!' said Finn angrily. As soon as the words had left his lips, he wished he hadn't said them. The pain in Adam's eyes was clear for anyone to see. Finn was confused. Adam was an android. Finn could beat him until he was exhausted and Adam would feel no pain at all. But here he was clearly hurt by a few angry words.

'I... I'm...' Finn began, but no more words came out.

'You're free,' said Adam, getting up. His voice was flat and he avoided looking Finn in the eye. 'But before you go, just listen to that noise, Finn. It's a drone. It uses a camera to see the heat of your body as it hunts you, and it's getting closer every minute. If you want to carry on alone, I won't stop you. They will kill you, of course, but you can choose to die if you wish. Or...' Adam paused for a second, 'you can come with me and hope that I don't cut your throat.'

Finn nodded slowly.

'I'll take that nod as a "yes", shall I? Oh, don't look so worried, Finn, I'm not actually going to cut your throat.'

Finn looked into Adam's eyes, and felt ashamed. Adam had done nothing to hurt him. Whatever Adam was, Finn knew he was telling the truth about one thing: Finn couldn't survive for more than an hour on his own. Adam was his only chance of staying alive and finding Ellie.

'Come on, then, Finn,' said Adam. 'There's a river nearby. We need to get to it – and quickly, too. I hope you can hold your breath for a long time.'

Finn looked at him with wide eyes. 'What?' he said.

'Never mind! I'll explain later. Quick, let's go. This way.'

Adam turned and began running deeper into the forest. Finn followed, the sound of the drone ringing in his ears.

CHAPTER EIGHT

The Hunt

The river was only minutes away. As they came to the edge of the trees, Adam stopped and looked around, and then threw down his bag.

'We have to be careful now,' he whispered. 'The drone is no more than a kilometre away. We have to make sure that their camera can't see the heat coming off your body. You're going to have to get under the water and hold your breath for as long as you can. The water should be cold enough to hide your body heat, so they won't be able to find you.'

'I don't know if I'll be able to hold my breath long enough,' Finn said.

'Well, if you can't, we're in trouble,' said Adam. 'There's no choice, Finn. You've got to try. I'll be with you.'

'All right. Let's do it.'

Once they left the trees, they ran as fast as they could and slid into the water. Finn gasped. The water was colder than he'd imagined.

'I can hear it – it's very close! Quick, take a breath now!' said Adam as he pushed Finn's head under. Finn just had time to fill his chest with as much air as possible before the water closed over his head.

The river was wide and flowed fast, collecting dirt as it went, and dropping it lower down the valley. It almost seemed alive the way it pushed hard against Finn's legs. He had to use all his power to keep his feet fixed to the ground.

But with every second, he felt weaker. It was so hard holding his breath. The need to breathe grew stronger and stronger. It made his head feel light and his legs began to tremble. He knew he couldn't carry on much longer.

Finn could see the dark shape of Adam nearby. He put out his hand to grab Adam's arm, but a stone moved under his foot and he fell backwards. His head hit a rock and he opened his mouth to cry with the pain. The water saw its chance and rushed in. He fought to rise up, to reach the fresh air, but a hand on his chest held him under. *So this is*

Finn fought to rise up, but a hand on his chest held him under.

what drowning feels like, Finn thought. He closed his eyes and saw Ellie's face. She was saying something to him, but he couldn't hear. And then everything went black.

Finn woke up coughing and gasping. Someone was hitting him hard on his back, and he could taste the river in his mouth.

'You're alive!' Adam was kneeling beside him, smiling. 'I don't mind telling you, Finn, that I'm relieved. For a minute, I thought I'd made a mistake, that—'

'You... you tried to kill me!' Finn coughed. He tried to move away, but his head hurt too much and he was weak.

'You probably won't believe me, but I was actually trying to save you, Finn. The drone was flying above us just as you tried to get out of the water. I had to keep you under, or it was the end for both of us.'

'That was... that was nearly the end for me anyway!' gasped Finn.

'It *was* frightening, it's true,' said Adam, 'but I judged it was a chance worth taking. And look, you're alive and accusing me of attempting to murder you once again! So everything is back to normal, right?' He laughed.

Finn coughed out some more water and smiled weakly.

'Thanks, Adam,' he said finally.

Adam smiled, but there was sadness in his eyes, too.

'We can't stay here talking,' he continued. 'It's getting light now, and they won't be too far away. There's a cave not far from here where we can hide while you rest.' He paused and looked at the back of Finn's head. 'And that's a nasty cut you've got there. We'll need to clean it.'

Adam carried Finn in his arms the whole way. When they reached the cave, he laid him down gently in the furthest corner.

'Here, you're shaking with cold,' Adam said, as he pulled a small blanket from his bag and covered Finn with it. 'I don't think it would be a good idea to light a fire yet, but this will keep you a bit warm.' He then took out a bottle of water, some matches, a first-aid kit, and some cheese and bread.

'First, I'll clean your wound, and then we'll eat something.'

'Wow, you think of everything!' Finn said.

'Yes, I'm clever like that,' Adam replied, and again Finn could see the shadow of sadness in his eyes.

'You have feelings, don't you?' Finn suddenly said.

Adam stopped what he was doing and looked at Finn. He nodded.

'How is that possible? I mean, you said androids don't have emotions and... and...'

'And I'm an android, a *machine*,' said Adam, finishing Finn's thought. Finn looked uncomfortable.

'I'm sorry. It was wrong of me to say that. I was upset and confused. I thought I could trust you to tell me the truth, then I wasn't so sure.'

'I never lied to you,' said Adam.

'No, I suppose not, but you didn't tell me the whole truth. You still haven't.'

Adam sighed. 'There wasn't enough time.'

'There is now,' said Finn. 'Please, Adam. What is the experiment you talked about? And where... where are my real parents?'

Adam sat back against the sharp wall of the cave and stared into the dark.

'I don't know what happened to your real parents. You were taken from your mother not long after you were born. By that time, androids had grown powerful and had begun to control much of the world. Most humans, I'm afraid, were killed, although some were kept alive as workers and for experiments.' Adam paused. 'Are you OK, Finn? Do you want me to continue?'

'Yes,' Finn whispered.

'Androids developed an experiment using children to understand the power of the human mind. They realized, you see, that while androids are more intelligent, they have something missing. They can't solve all problems with simple maths.'

Adam stopped and turned to look at Finn.

'You've probably noticed that I'm saying "they" when I talk about androids. That's because I don't consider myself to be an android. I'm not human either, of course. I'm in between. A freak. I am nothing.'

'No, Adam, don't say that!' Finn shouted.

Adam smiled.

'It's true, I'm afraid. I am neither one thing nor the other. You see, I was part of the experiment, too. They studied the minds of the human children and then put all the information into the android children. Twice a year, we were upgraded. Didn't you think it was strange that I went away on so many school trips and came back taller and stronger?'

'No,' said Finn, shaking his head. 'No, I didn't notice. You were always my clever, big brother. It seemed normal that you got bigger and cleverer.'

Adam laughed.

'The thing is, my intelligence developed a lot, but so did my emotions. I didn't like it at first – being angry and feeling jealous. Feelings aren't always good, are they? Mine often felt like there were a million pieces of broken glass cutting me from inside here.' Adam put his hand where his heart would be if he were human.

'Jealous?' asked Finn. 'Who could *you* possibly be jealous of?'

'You, of course!'

'Me?' Finn's eyes opened wide with surprise. 'Why would you be jealous of me? You can do everything better than I can.'

'You know, Finn, sometimes it's hard to remember you are a human – you have so little understanding of emotions! I was jealous because our "parents" were more interested in you, because you were so important to the experiment. And because you were free to play music and draw and write stories all day at school. I desperately wanted to do these things, too, but I wasn't allowed. All the androids went to Highway Academy and spent every day working with *Serveworld*. The upgrades were aimed at helping us solve problems, nothing else. And the androids didn't understand the new feelings that we were starting to have, like being happy or not.'

While Adam was speaking, Finn's face had begun to burn

a bright red.

'I was jealous of you, too,' Finn said softly. 'I hated every minute of creative writing class, of painting all afternoon, and playing the guitar really badly. I wanted to learn maths and science, and I was so angry that you could use *Serveworld* and I couldn't!'

'Yeah, I guessed that,' Adam said, laughing.

'And I thought you didn't like me very much. It's true, our "parents" were always asking me questions, but you didn't seem interested in anything I said. And you often called me stupid and weak...'

'I'm sorry about that,' said Adam. 'I really am. When my emotions started to grow stronger, I didn't have a lot of control over them. It was so frightening. Sometimes I just wanted to hurt someone for no reason at all. Usually it was you!' He lit a match and looked into Finn's face.

'So why didn't you tell me any of this?' asked Finn. 'Did you always know?'

'I've known for a long time, yes, but it was only when I began to *feel* that it seemed important. By then, of course, I realized how dangerous it was for you. Fortunately, I was able to hack the rebels' computer system to find others who were like me. That's how I discovered the rebels and contacted them.'

'But aren't *all* the others like you? I mean the others in Highway Academy. Don't they all want to escape?'

'That's the interesting thing, Finn, the thing none of the androids expected. We all received regular upgrades and we all have emotions, but the feelings aren't all the same.

They lead us to different experiences. Some want to feel the excitement of power, and others just want to find someone to love.'

They were silent for a moment, and then Finn moved closer to Adam. 'Don't ever say you're nothing again, Adam. You're everything to me. You're all the family I have.'

Finn watched as a tear fell from Adam's eye.

'You're everything to me. You're all the family I have.'

CHAPTER NINE
The Fight

Adam bent over Finn and shook him gently.

'Come on, sleepyhead! It's dark outside. It's time for us to go.'

Finn opened his eyes, but couldn't see the smile on Adam's face. The cave was as dark as thick, black oil. For a moment, he had no idea where he was. He sat up quickly.

'Ouch!'

'Take it easy! You're injured, remember?' said Adam.

Finn felt the cut on the back of his head. In a second, everything that had happened over the last three days came rushing back to him. It was like a film playing inside his head at high speed.

'What time is it?' he asked.

'Just after midnight.' Adam lit a match to help Finn get up safely. 'If we leave now, we'll have more than enough time to reach the lake before it's light. The rebels will be there with a boat ready to take us to the other side.'

'Are the rebels all... I mean, are they...?' Finn hesitated. 'All like me?'

Finn nodded.

'No, there are humans, too, though not many.'

Finn thought about his parents, his real parents. Had they died with all the others?

'Rebel groups attack prison hospitals where they know the androids are holding humans,' Adam continued, 'and then they take the humans back to the rebel city.'

'What do you mean, "prison hospitals?"' said Finn, his eyes shining like a cat's in the dying light of the match. 'I don't like the sound of that.'

'No one does, Finn. It's where they do more experiments, and it's all a lot worse than The Room, believe me.'

Finn felt a cold wave of fear pass through him. He started shaking. Adam lit another match and held it near to Finn's face.

'Are you OK?'

'I'm not sure. I was wondering about Ellie. Oh Adam, do you think they've taken her to one of those?'

Adam put an arm around Finn's shoulders.

'We can't think about that now. When we get to the rebel city, we'll be able to find out more. Our aim now is to get to safety. If we don't do that, we won't be any use to Ellie or anyone else. Agreed?'

Finn thought for a moment. 'Agreed.'

'All right, then. Are you ready?'

'I guess so.'

'Are you sure? Is your head too painful?' Adam was clearly worried about him.

'No, no, it's nothing like that,' said Finn softly. His throat was suddenly very dry. 'It's just that I'm… I'm sorry, Adam, but I'm afraid.'

'Well,' said Adam gently, 'I'm a little afraid, too, but I know that everything's going to be fine. We're going to get to the rebel city and start a new life. We'll make a new family together – just you and me, I promise.'

Adam smiled. Finn tried hard to smile as well, but he knew that this time it would be hard for Adam to keep his promise.

Adam guided Finn out of the cave where the full moon gave them more light.

'Follow me, keep close, and try to be as quiet as you can,' Adam whispered.

Finn did as he was told, though being quiet wasn't so easy. There had not been much rain for weeks and the leaves and branches were as dry as a bone. With every step Finn took, they broke loudly under his feet and made him look around anxiously. Although Adam was bigger and stronger, he moved more quickly and more lightly.

'Shh, Finn!' Adam said. 'Can't you make less noise?'

'I'm trying.'

Adam sighed. 'I'll have to carry you, I think.'

Finn shook his head. 'No, I'll be fine. I'll try harder.'

But Adam didn't listen. Before Finn could say another word, he swung him onto his back and they carried on with their journey.

The way was steep at first, but Adam didn't slow down for a second. He moved through the trees as easily as any wild cat. Finn held on to Adam's neck and watched as the forest slid by. He thought about Ellie. Where was she? Would anyone know where she'd been taken? Adam had told him that the rebels had hacked the computer systems of the androids many times. It was one of the reasons why they had so much information about the experiments on humans, and about where the prison hospitals were.

Androids like Adam, who had had upgrades from the studies on human children, often understood more about computers than others. Some of them, however, chose to hide the fact in order to help the rebels. His brother was, after all, a kind of spy! Finn felt very proud.

After what seemed like hours, Adam stopped and put Finn down.

'The lake is just over there,' whispered Adam. He pointed, and Finn could see the moon shining on the black water. 'The rebels are waiting for us on the beach a few hundred metres away. There aren't many trees from here to the lake, though, so we won't have much cover. I think we'd better wait a little and watch, in case there's anyone else waiting for us!'

Finn nodded. He felt sick with excitement and fear. They were so close now. Soon they were going to be on a boat sailing towards a new future. He couldn't quite believe it was actually going to happen.

The minutes passed slowly. Everywhere was so still and quiet that even the sound of their breathing seemed loud. Nothing moved except the occasional branch waving in the gentle wind. It felt like Finn and Adam were the only ones left in the world.

'Come on, Finn,' said Adam at last. 'I think it's safe to go. Follow me and stay close to the trees. All right?'

'All right.'

They kept their heads low as they moved. Finn could see Adam searching the lake's edge for a sign that the rebels were waiting for them.

'It's time to move out of the trees and cross the beach, Finn. Are you ready?'

'I've never been more ready in my life!'

Adam smiled. 'Me neither. Soon, we'll know what freedom means.' He took a deep breath. 'Come on, then, let's go.'

They ran from the shadow of the trees onto the soft ground of the beach. Finn saw a light flashing from the lake. *That must be the rebels*, he thought, relieved to see that they were very close indeed. He opened his mouth to call out softly to Adam, and that was when he felt a sharp pain in his back.

'Aargh!' he screamed as he fell to his knees.

Adam swung round.

'Finn!' he shouted. 'Are you all right?'

Finn could hear running feet behind him.

'Go, Adam. They're here. Run!'

Finn watched the expression on Adam's face change as he realized that his brother had been hit.

'It's all over, Adam,' a woman's voice said from behind. 'Come quietly and we won't have to hurt you.'

Finn knew that voice. It was Miss Edwards.

'Is that you, Miss—'

'Shut up, Finn!' she hissed, and her boot pushed down hard on his shoulder so that he fell flat onto his stomach. She was holding a weapon. It looked like a smooth stick in the dark, but then Finn saw the end of it burn with an orange light. It was a laser, he realized, and it was what had hit him.

'Drop your bag and put your hands high where I can see

them,' she said to Adam.

'Please don't hurt my brother!' said Adam, letting his bag slide to the ground.

'Brother?' Miss Edwards said. 'You really are a freak, aren't you? That's what humans would call you, Adam.'

'Please don't hurt my brother!' said Adam.

'Don't listen to her, Adam! Don't do what she says!' shouted Finn. 'Run!'

Miss Edwards bent to hit Finn across his head, and that was all the time Adam needed to pull his own laser from his bag. He lifted it high above his head. A lightning flash jumped from the weapon to Miss Edwards as Adam pointed it at her neck. She fell to the ground and lay still.

'Quick, Finn, run!' said Adam. 'I'll wait and check for any others and then I'll follow.'

'I'm not going without you,' said Finn.

'Don't be stupid, Finn,' said Adam. Finn hesitated, but Adam pushed him forwards. 'I can hear another one coming. Just go!'

Finn ran as fast as he had ever done in his life. His legs worked harder and harder, and he was breathing so heavily that he didn't hear the sound of feet behind him. He didn't need to hear. The hairs on the back of his neck were standing up – he knew that someone or something was close by.

The android came at him from behind, throwing him up into the air. He gasped like a fish out of water as he fell onto his back on the ground. The android put a knee calmly on Finn's chest to stop him getting up. His hand fastened around Finn's throat and he bent forwards. His face was very close to Finn's as he spoke.

'You humans are so stupid. Don't you know that you can never beat us – not at running, not at anything?'

'That's where you're wrong!' shouted Finn. He had grabbed a rock when he fell, and he now used all his power to hit the android's head with it. The android silently slid off Finn's body, its head swinging from its neck.

Finn got up, trembling from head to foot. He turned to where he'd left Adam, but it was still too dark to see anything. He opened his mouth to call Adam's name, but a hand closed over it.

'You can't help him now, Finn,' a voice said softly in his ear. 'It's too late. Your brother is dead, I'm afraid. I'm so sorry. We're going to take you to the rebel city where you'll be safe.'

Finn opened his mouth to call Adam's name,
but a hand closed over it.

CHAPTER TEN

Together Again

Finn woke up in bed. There were machines on both sides of him, and tubes coming out of his arm. The room he was in had neither a clock nor a window, so he didn't know if it was day or night. On the other side of the door, he could hear movement and bits of conversation that came and went like distant thunder.

He sat up and looked around. He was wearing a long grey hospital shirt. Where was he? His heart started to beat fast. *This is a prison hospital,* he thought; *I have to get out of here.* Without pausing, he pulled the tubes from his arm, feeling the sharp pain as they came out. He stood shakily on the cold floor. The machines immediately started flashing and sounding an alarm. He moved weakly towards the door, but before he could take more than a few steps, it was thrown open and a young man and woman entered, followed by a nurse. Finn froze.

'Now then, Finn, where do you think you're going?' said the woman, smiling. 'It's too soon for you to be out of bed. You need to rest a while longer.' Her eyes were kind. Finn was confused.

'Yes, you've had a rough time, Finn,' said the man.

Finn looked from one to the other. He had a feeling he had seen them before, but where?

'Why don't you lie back on the bed?' said the woman, and the nurse moved forwards and took his arm. He felt too

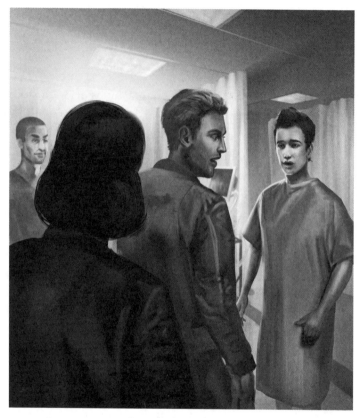

A young man and woman entered, followed by a nurse.

weak and tired to fight, and suddenly he had the strongest feeling that nothing mattered, nothing at all.

'You know, it's normal not to remember very much after a big shock, Finn,' the woman said. 'Sometimes it makes people forget for a short while.'

Shock? What shock? Finn searched his mind. What had happened? Who were these people?

'Don't you remember anything about escaping?' asked the man. 'The lake? The fight?'

'Careful!' said the woman. 'Don't say too much too soon. He needs time.'

Finn stared at them. Pictures started to appear in his mind. He remembered a boat. It was dark and two people – these two people! – were pulling him onto it.

'I was crying,' Finn suddenly said. 'Why was I crying?'

The man and the woman looked at each other, but before they could say anything, tears started to fall from Finn's eyes. 'Adam,' he said softly. 'My brother is dead!'

The woman came and put her arm around him. 'Yes, Adam is dead,' she said gently. 'He was very brave, and his greatest wish was to bring you to safety.'

Finn put his head in his hands and let his tears fall.

'I'd only just found him,' he sobbed. 'I mean, he'd always been there, but I'd never realized how much I cared for him. Or that he cared for me. We were going to have a new start and then...' He stopped, unable to describe what had happened.

The man stepped forward. 'There was quite a battle after we found Adam,' he said. 'All those who had hunted you are now terminated. We were also able to bring Adam's body back.'

'Thank you,' Finn whispered.

'Here in the rebel city,' continued the woman, 'even we androids like to bury those who we have lost. When you are better, and ready, we can bury Adam.'

Finn nodded.

'There is one more thing,' added the man. 'When Adam contacted us a couple of days ago, he asked us to look for your friend Ellie. She was taken from school by the secret police – is that correct?'

'Yes!' Finn felt excitement rush like blood through his body. He had almost lost hope of seeing Ellie ever again.

'Well, we've had some good luck. She was found during an attack on a prison hospital a few days ago. She is well, and the nurses are caring for her in another room. You can see her when you're feeling better.'

'I want to see her now!' Finn dried the tears on his face. 'Please! I've lost everyone and everything else.'

The man shook his head, but the woman hesitated. 'I think it'll do no harm,' she said to the man. 'In fact, it will be good for him. Hope is always a good thing.'

They left Finn with the nurse, to fix the tubes and make him comfortable once more. The minutes waiting seemed like hours to him, but finally, the door opened and there she stood.

'Ellie!' he said softly.

She ran to him and threw her arms around his neck. 'Oh Finn, I thought I'd never see you again!'

Her eyes were filled with tears, and Finn brushed them away.

'You know, I think that's the first time I've seen you cry,' Finn said.

'Seriously? Well, I haven't stopped crying since they took me away. I thought they were going to kill me, and when I found out that they were all androids – all of them, our

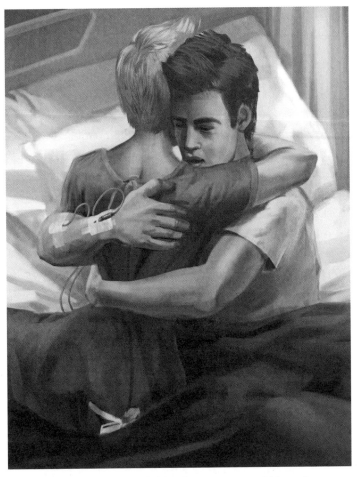

Ellie ran to Finn and threw her arms around his neck.

parents, the teachers, Adam – I almost wished they would.'

'Adam isn't – wasn't – like the others,' Finn said sharply.

'Yes, I know that now. He was trying to save us, and I'm so sorry he... well, that he's gone.'

Finn bent his head and took a deep breath in order to stop more tears coming.

'How did you find out?'

'About Adam? When I was brought here, they told me.'

'No, I mean about the adults being androids. They took you away because you knew, didn't they?'

'Yes, but I didn't know everything. Remember the day I was off school with a cold?' Finn nodded. 'Well, "Mum" left *Serveworld* unlocked while she made me lunch, and I managed to take a look. There was stuff on it about the work she was doing for this big experiment. Stuff about me. I didn't read much of it because I didn't have time, but it was enough to make me really frightened.'

'Did you suspect your parents were androids, too?'

'No. Well, yes. Oh Finn, I didn't want to believe it was true. It was all a great shock. But we were both beginning to see that there were a lot of things that just weren't right in our lives, weren't we?'

'Yeah, that's true. But what happened next? How did they find out that you knew?'

'Oh Finn, I was really stupid. You see, I'd been keeping a diary for years.'

'You never told me!'

'It was my thing, my secret. Anyway, you hated writing so much I didn't think you'd understand. I hid the diary under a floorboard in my bedroom. It had been safe there for so long. But that night, I was so upset about what I'd found out that I didn't put the board back in the right place. "Mum" found it the next morning.'

'So that's why they came to school for you?'

'Yes. I had no idea that they'd discovered it. I'd been hoping that we would escape together that evening.'

'Instead it was me and Adam who tried to escape,' said Finn, his voice shaking.

'I'm so sorry about your brother, Finn. I really am. But I can't tell you how relieved I am that you're here. I thought about you all the time in the prison hospital, you know. It was awful in there.' Ellie paused and looked away. Finn could feel her hands trembling in his.

'You don't have to talk about it if you don't want to, Ellie.'

'I know, but it helps to tell you.' She took a deep breath before continuing.

'They fixed all kinds of tubes to me and I had to wear a headset the whole time. I felt like I was dreaming – but the dreams were more like horror films. Sometimes they used electricity to hurt me.'

Ellie began to sob and Finn held her close.

'Shh. It's OK now. We're safe here.'

'Yes. Thankfully, the rebels came. One minute I was lying on a bed in pain, and the next I was running down a hall with smoke everywhere. They'd planted a bomb and destroyed most of the side of the building!'

'I saw you!' Finn shouted. 'There was the sound of a bomb exploding and clouds of smoke.'

'What do you mean? How could you see me? You weren't there!'

'No, but I was sent to The Room the day they took you. I

saw it all happen. Honestly, I saw it all.'

They looked at each other in silence for a moment.

'I think they were sending my thoughts to you in some way,' Ellie said.

'Yeah, another of their little experiments!' cried Finn.

'Well, they knew I'd discovered part of their secret—'

'And they also knew we were best friends,' continued Finn. 'Perhaps they wanted to know if I would feel horror at your pain. Well, they were right. I did.'

Ellie reached for Finn's hand and held it in hers. After all that had happened to them, nothing was too extraordinary to be true.

'It's just you and me now, Ellie,' Finn said finally. 'We have to start again here, together.'

'Yes,' Ellie said. She sighed. The last few days had left her feeling exhausted. Everything and everyone she had ever known was gone. All except Finn.

'We have to fight for a different future here where androids and humans live together and try to make a new world – a better world,' Finn said.

'Yes,' she said after a moment. 'And I'm so thankful to Adam. He brought you back to me—'

'And gave us a chance to be free,' said Finn, finishing Ellie's thought. It was an old habit they had.

android *(n)* a type of machine that looks like a real person

anxious *(adj)* worried and afraid

attack *(v & n)* to start fighting or hurting somebody or something

choice *(n)* when you choose between two or more people or things

churchyard *(n)* the area of land around a church where dead people are buried

cough *(v)* to send air out of your mouth and chest with a sudden loud noise

creative *(adj)* using a lot of imagination and new ideas

draw *(v)* to pull something out

drone *(n)* a machine that flies in the air without a pilot, but is controlled by someone on the ground; it is often used to carefully watch a person or a place

emotion *(n)* something that you experience or feel, for example love, fear, or happiness

experiment *(n)* a test that you do to learn something or to see if something is true

faint *(v)* to suddenly be unable to see, feel, or think for a short time, and perhaps to fall down, usually because you are weak, ill, or injured

feeling *(n)* something that you feel or experience, usually for a short time, for example, love, fear, or happiness / an idea that you are not certain about

flash *(v & n)* to shine brightly for a very short time, or to shine on and off again and again very quickly

freak *(n)* a person who looks strange, or is unusual or different from other people

gasp *(v)* to breathe in suddenly, for example because you are in pain or are surprised

grab *(v)* to take something in a rough and sudden way

grave *(n)*　a hole in the ground where a dead person's body is buried

hack *(v)*　to use a computer to get into somebody else's computer in order to damage it or get secret information

headset *(n)*　something that you wear on your head with special parts for speaking into and for listening to music, radio programmes, etc.

hiss *(v)*　to say something in a low, angry voice

hunt *(v & n)*　to chase animals to kill them

joke *(n & v)*　something that you say or do to make people laugh

keyboard *(n)*　the part of a computer that has lots of very small buttons that you press with your fingers to enter information

maths *(n)*　(mathematics) the study of numbers and shapes

mind *(n)*　the part of you that thinks, knows, and remembers

nod *(v & n)*　to move your head down and up again quickly, usually because you agree with or understand something

password *(n)*　a secret word, or a group of letters and numbers, that allows you to go into a place or start using a computer

power *(n)*　the ability to be strong, when you are able to control people or things; **powerful** *(adj)*

rebel *(v & n)*　to fight against the people who are in control, for example parents or leaders

relieved *(adj)*　being happy because a problem, danger, or worry has now gone

rush *(v)*　to move or do something very quickly

safety *(n)*　a place or situation where there is no danger

science *(n)*　the study of the natural world

sentence *(n)*　a group of words, usually with a verb, that tells you something; it begins with a capital letter and usually ends with a full stop

shock *(n)*　a very bad surprise

sigh *(v)* to breathe out slowly making a long soft sound, for example because you are sad, tired, or pleased

sob *(v)* to cry loudly, making short sounds

strict *(adj)* If you are strict, you make people do what you want, and do not allow them to behave badly.

stuff *(n)* any group of things, for example pieces of information

swing *(v)* to move backwards and forwards or from side to side through the air

teenager *(n)* a person who is between thirteen and nineteen years old

terminate *(v)* to kill; to end, or to make something end

throat *(n)* the front part of your neck, which takes food and air down from your mouth into your body

trillion *(num)* one million million; 1,000,000,000,000

trust *(v)* to believe that somebody is honest and good

tube *(n)* a long thin pipe that something can move through, for example gas

type *(v)* to write something using a machine that has keys or small buttons, like a computer or a typewriter

upgrade *(v & n)* to change something, for example a computer or other machine, for a different one which is better

upset *(adj)* feeling unhappy or worried

warden *(n)* a person who looks after a place and the people in it for their job

Intelligent machines

When was the first machine built? Who dreamed of making the first computer? The history of machines is surprisingly long. And from the earliest days, people have wanted to make a machine that looks, 'thinks', or behaves like a person – a machine with Artificial Intelligence (AI).

Here are a few steps that have been taken towards the future of Artificial Intelligence.

2,500 BC It was the Greeks who first thought about trying to create a machine that would look like a person. In their stories and writing, the Greeks described automatons: machines that look and move like a human or animal. The word *automaton* is a Greek word meaning 'self-moving'.

1495 Leonardo da Vinci drew an automaton called 'the robotic knight' that looked like a fifteenth-century soldier. The automaton could stand, sit, and move its arms. Many years later, in 2002, the scientist Mark Rosheim used da Vinci's drawings to build a real 'robotic knight' – and he found that it actually could move in the way da Vinci had planned. Rosheim then used the same five-hundred-year-old drawings to build new robots.

1820s–1871 Charles Babbage, a British mathematician, is often described as the father of the computer. He made plans for a machine called the Difference Engine, which was able to do difficult maths, and, later, for one called the Analytical Engine, which could also 'remember' the maths. Babbage never built these machines himself, but in 1991, the Science Museum in London was able to use his plans to build a Difference Engine.

1943–45 Alan Turing, another British mathematician, helped to make the first modern computer during World War Two. Turing also suggested a test which can recognize an intelligent machine. His test said that a machine is intelligent if it can make a human believe they are talking to another human. The Turing test has been very important in ideas about Artificial Intelligence.

2014 A computer called Eugene became the first to pass the Turing test at the University of Reading. Eugene was able to make people believe they were talking to a thirteen-year-old boy.

READ & RESEARCH Read 'Beyond the Story', and research the answers to these questions.

1 Find out about a scientist who has been important in developing AI.

2 Find two examples of how AI is used in our lives today. Then find an idea that you think is exciting for how we may use it in the future.

robot *(n)* a machine that can do work by itself – often work that humans do

Think Ahead

1 Read about the story on the back cover. Choose the correct word/phrase to complete the sentences.

1 This is *a funny / an adventure* story.

2 The story is about some *students / teachers* at Mangrove High School.

3 At Mangrove, the students do *a lot of / no* maths.

4 Students go to The Room because they *have to / want to*.

2 Read the back cover and the chapter titles. What do you think is going to happen in the story? Tick (✔) the sentences you think are true.

1 Finn and Ellie are going to be separated.

2 Finn is going to run away from home.

3 Finn and Ellie are going to move to a new school.

4 Ellie is going to buy a computer.

5 Someone is going to spend time in The Room.

3 **RESEARCH** Before you read, find the answers to these questions.

1 This story is about a time in the future. Who wrote the books *Brave New World* and *The Time Machine*, which were also about a time in the future?

2 In which book about the future can you find Room 101 and the Thought Police – and what are they?

Chapter Check

CHAPTER 1 Are the sentences true or false?

1 Finn had always been a rebel.

2 Everyone was frightened of The Wardens.

3 Ellie didn't mind going to The Room.

4 Students were only sent to The Room as a punishment.

5 Finn thought that he and Ellie were in a school for children who weren't clever.

CHAPTER 2 Match the sentence halves.

1 Finn had tried many times…

2 Finn didn't want Adam…

3 Finn knew that his parents were going…

4 Finn wanted his parents…

a to show more interest in Adam.

b to tell his parents that he had been using *Serveworld*.

c to discover the password to *Serveworld*.

d to ask him lots of questions about The Room.

CHAPTER 3 Complete the sentences with the adjectives.

careful   frightened   surprised   worried

1 Ellie was _____ when she heard her parents arguing.

2 Ellie always bit her lip when she was _____.

3 Finn and Ellie were always _____ when they arrived at the churchyard.

4 Finn and Ellie were _____ when they saw something behind the graves.

CHAPTER 4 Choose the correct answers.

1 Finn couldn't get to sleep because he was...
   a worried about Ellie.
   b excited about seeing Ellie in the morning.

2 Finn wanted to go to school because...
   a he was beginning to enjoy it.
   b he wanted to see Ellie.

3 Finn's visit to The Room was worse than before...
   a because he was already afraid when he got there.
   b because he was angry Miss Edwards caught him.

4 Adam was a 'mystery' to Finn because...
   a he was always very controlled.
   b he changed from nice to angry to calm.

CHAPTER 5 Tick (✓) the three sentences which are true.

1 Ellie was absent from school because she'd discovered something dangerous. ☐
2 Ellie behaved strangely during the morning at school. ☐
3 Miss Edwards called The Wardens to take Ellie away. ☐
4 Finn had a frightening dream about Ellie in The Room. ☐
5 Finn decided that he needed to look for Ellie. ☐

CHAPTER 6 Match the sentence halves.

1 Adam hadn't told Finn about the experiment before…
2 Adam had followed Finn and Ellie to the churchyard…
3 The National Home Guard were near the churchyard…
4 Adam had decided to fight with the rebels…

a because the rebels were starting to attack places close to the town.
b because he wanted to make sure they were safe from the National Home Guard.
c because he didn't want androids to do experiments on people.
d because it was dangerous to know.

CHAPTER 7 Put the events in order.

a Finn heard the sound of a drone.

b Adam decided to carry Finn on his back.

c Finn realized that Adam was an android.

d Adam persuaded Finn to trust him again.

e Finn left Adam and ran into the forest.

CHAPTER 8 Are the sentences true or false?

1 Adam tried to kill Finn in the river.

2 Finn's real parents were probably killed after he was born.

3 Adam was not really an android or a human.

4 When Adam was upgraded, he developed emotions.

5 The upgraded androids all had the same emotions.

CHAPTER 8 Correct the underlined words.

1 When Finn fell in the river, he cut his <u>arm</u>.

2 When Adam held Finn under the water, he was trying to <u>kill</u> him.

3 Adam was <u>pleased</u> because Finn was free to play music and draw and write stories all day.

4 Adam hacked the <u>androids'</u> computer system to find others who were like him.

CHAPTER 9 Complete the sentences with the places below.

beach   forest   prison hospitals   rebel city

1 Androids did experiments on humans in the
_____.

2 Adam hoped that they could start a new life in the
_____.

3 Finn found it difficult to move quietly in the
_____.

4 Adam and Finn were attacked on the _____.

CHAPTER 10 Choose the correct words.

1 When Finn woke up, he *remembered / didn't remember* what happened at the lake.

2 When the man and woman came into the room, Finn *knew / didn't know* who they were.

3 The androids Adam and Finn fought with at the beach *all ran away / were all terminated.*

4 When Ellie was in the prison hospital, she thought she was going to *die / escape.*

5 Ellie's 'mum' discovered what she knew when she found it in *Serveworld / a diary.*

6 Ellie escaped from the prison hospital because there was a *bomb / fire.*

Focus on Vocabulary

1 Complete the sentences with the correct words.

fainted flashed grabbed hacked typed

1 Finn was so frightened of small, silent places that he
_____ when he was in The Room.

2 The android was going to hurt Finn, but Finn
_____ a rock and hit it on the head.

3 The rebels had _____ the androids' computer
systems many times.

4 When Finn and Adam got close to the lake, the rebels
_____ a light.

5 Finn _____ EX7*O@/ into Adam's computer,
but it was not the right password.

2 Complete the crossword.

Across
2 to move very quickly
5 very surprised

Down
1 to believe someone
3 unhappy and sad
4 to cry loudly

Focus on Language

1 **Complete the text with the correct form of the verbs. Use the past perfect simple, past perfect continuous, or present perfect continuous.**

Finn ¹_____ (try) for months to discover Adam's password, but it ²_____ (not be) easy to watch his fingers as he typed it in. When at last he ³_____ (get) the password right, it ⁴_____ (be) a terrible disappointment. He ⁵_____ (not understand) anything on the screen. 'I ⁶_____ (wait) all this time,' he thought, 'and for nothing.'

2 **DECODE** **Look at the sentences and decide where you would put the words in italics on the line below.**

1 It was a *rather* difficult exercise.

very difficult ●————————●————————●————————● easy

2 She didn't *quite* understand how to do the question.

understand well ●————————●————————●————————● not understand

3 'I *absolutely* hate maths!' she said.

hate ●————————●————————●————————● like

4 'I don't agree,' said her friend. 'I think it's *quite* fun.'

lots of fun ●————————●————————●————————● not fun

5 'I *absolutely* agree,' said her teacher.

agree ●————————●————————●————————● not agree

3 **DECODE** **Write three sentences using the words above.**

Discussion

1 Write four questions for your partner, as below, and then take turns asking and answering.

   Student A: Write two questions about the characters in the story and two questions about the themes in the story.

   Student B: Write two questions about the ending of the story and two questions about what will happen next.

2 Choose your favourite chapter from the story and complete the sentences below.

   My favourite part of the story is chapter _____ because it is _____. When I read this chapter, I *thought / felt / understood* _____.

3 **COMMUNICATE** In one minute, tell your partner about the chapter. Then tell them why it is your favourite.

4 **THINK CRITICALLY** Discuss one of the questions below with your partner. Do you agree? Use the phrases below.

   I agree / don't agree.   I think so too.   I think that…
   I'm not so sure about that.   Yes, but don't you think…

   a In your opinion, why did Finn and Ellie suddenly begin to notice that there was something strange about their parents?

   b Do you think it was correct to say that Adam 'died'? Is it better to say that he 'was terminated'?

PROJECT

1 Read the story description and match it to one of the book covers below.

A human being is soft and weak. It needs air, water, and food to survive. It spends a third of its life asleep, and can't work if the temperature is too hot or too cold. But a robot is made of metal. It uses the power of electricity, never sleeps, and can work in any temperature. It is stronger and sometimes more human than human beings.

A    B    C

2 **THINK CRITICALLY** In groups, think of your own story about a future world. Think about these questions.

Who are the main characters?

Where does the story happen?

What is special or unusual about this future world?

What happens in the story?

3 **COLLABORATE & CREATE** In groups, create a book cover and description using the example in exercise 1 and the ideas in exercise 2.

4 **COMMUNICATE** In groups, present your book covers and story descriptions to the class.

If you liked this Bookworm, why not try...

The Thirty-Nine Steps

STAGE 4

John Buchan, retold by Nick Bullard

'I turned on the light, but there was nobody there. Then I saw something in the corner that made my blood turn cold. Scudder was lying on his back. There was a long knife through his heart, pinning him to the floor.' Soon Richard Hannay is running for his life across the hills of Scotland. The police are chasing him for a murder he did not do, and another, more dangerous enemy is chasing him as well – the mysterious 'Black Stone'. Who are these people? And why do they want Hannay dead?

Do Androids Dream of Electric Sheep?

STAGE 5

Philip K. Dick, retold by A. Hopkins and J. Potter

San Francisco lies under a cloud of radioactive dust. People live in half-deserted buildings, and keep electric animals as pets because many real animals have died. Most people emigrate to Mars – unless they have a job to do on Earth. Like Rick Deckard – android killer for the police and owner of an electric sheep. This week he has to find, identify, and kill six escaped androids. They're machines, but they look and sound and think like humans – clever, dangerous humans. The film *Blade Runner* was based on this famous novel.